A Note to Parents and Caregivers:

Read-it! Readers are for children who are just starting on the amazing road to reading. These beautiful books support both the acquisition of reading skills and the love of books.

 The PURPLE LEVEL presents basic topics and objects using high frequency words and simple language patterns.

 The RED LEVEL presents familiar topics using common words and repeating sentence patterns.

 The BLUE LEVEL presents new ideas using a larger vocabulary and varied sentence structure.

 The YELLOW LEVEL presents more challenging ideas, a broad vocabulary, and wide variety in sentence structure.

 The GREEN LEVEL presents more complex ideas, an extended vocabulary range, and expanded language structures.

 The ORANGE LEVEL presents a wide range of ideas and concepts using challenging vocabulary and complex language structures.

When sharing a book with your child, read in short stretches, pausing often to talk about the pictures. Have your child turn the pages and point to the pictures and familiar words. And be sure to reread favorite stories or parts of stories.

There is no right or wrong way to share books with children. Find time to read with your child, and pass on the legacy of literacy.

Adria F. Klein, Ph.D.
Professor Emeritus
California State University
San Bernardino, California

Editor: Christianne Jones
Designer: Nathan Gassman
Page Production: Lori Bye
Creative Director: Keith Griffin
Editorial Director: Carol Jones
The illustrations in this book were created digitally.

Picture Window Books
5115 Excelsior Boulevard
Suite 232
Minneapolis, MN 55416
877-845-8392
www.picturewindowbooks.com

Printed in the United States of America.

Library of Congress Cataloging-in-Publication Data
Hardy, Lorién Trover
The snow dance / by Lorién Trover Hardy ; illustrated by Zachary Trover.
p. cm. — (Read-it! readers)
Summary: Though they look ordinary during the day, Mac knows that his four
snowmen have a special nighttime secret.
ISBN-13: 978-1-4048-2421-8 (hardcover)
ISBN-10: 1-4048-2421-9 (hardcover)
[1. Snowmen—Fiction. 2. Magic—Fiction. 3. Dance—Fiction.] I. Trover, Zachary, ill.
II. Title. III. Series.

PZ7.H22144Sn 2006
[E]—dc22   2006003573

The Snow Dance

by Lorién Trover Hardy
illustrated by Zachary Trover

Special thanks to our advisers for their expertise:

Adria F. Klein, Ph.D.
Professor Emeritus, California State University
San Bernardino, California

Susan Kesselring, M.A.
Literacy Educator
Rosemount–Apple Valley–Eagan (Minnesota) School District

PICTURE WINDOW BOOKS
Minneapolis, Minnesota

Mac makes four perfect snowmen.

The first one wears a huge cowboy hat.

6

The second one wears a rainbow scarf.

9

The third one wears a hula skirt.

The fourth one wears a black-and-white checkered tie.

They look like average snowmen, but Mac knows a secret.

14

While everyone else sleeps, the snowmen dance. Mac stays up late and watches them.

The snowmen dance the tango through the trees.

They dance the mambo around the mailbox.

They dance the waltz by the window.
Soon, Mac falls asleep.

24

The snowmen dance and dance and dance.
They dance until the sun peeks over the hills.

25

Then, the snowmen hurry back to their places.

By morning, all of the snowmen are back
where Mac left them.

Nobody has any idea.

Nobody except Mac, that is.

More *Read-it!* Readers

Bright pictures and fun stories help you practice your reading skills. Look for more books at your level.

Bamboo at the Beach 1-4048-1035-8

The Best Lunch 1-4048-1578-3

Clinks the Robot 1-4048-1579-1

Eight Enormous Elephants 1-4048-0054-9

Flynn Flies High 1-4048-0563-X

Freddie's Fears 1-4048-0056-5

Loop, Swoop, and Pull! 1-4048-1611-9

Marvin, the Blue Pig 1-4048-0564-8

Mary and the Fairy 1-4048-0066-2

Megan Has to Move 1-4048-1613-5

Moo! 1-4048-0643-1

My Favorite Monster 1-4048-1029-3

Pippin's Big Jump 1-4048-0555-9

Pony Party 1-4048-1612-7

Rudy Helps Out 1-4048-2420-0

Sounds Like Fun 1-4048-0649-0

The Ticket 1-4048-2423-5

Tired of Waiting 1-4048-0650-4

Whose Birthday Is It? 1-4048-0554-0

Looking for a specific title or level? A complete list of *Read-it!* Readers is available on our Web site:

www.picturewindowbooks.com